Midni

MW01135824

Ops Series World (Crimson Ops)

by

Mandy M. Roth

Midnight Echoes: Part of the Immortal Ops Series World (Crimson Ops)© Copyright 2016, Mandy M. Roth
First Electronic Printing Oct 2016
Second Electronic Printing Dec 2016, Raven Happy Hour LLC
Trade Paperback Printing Dec 2016
ALL RIGHTS RESERVED.

All books are copyrighted to the author and may not be resold or given away without written permission from the author, Mandy M. Roth.

This novel is a work of fiction and intended for mature audiences only. Any and all characters, names, events, places and incidents are used under the umbrella of fiction and are of the author's imagination and should not be confused with fact. Any resemblance to persons, living or dead, or events or places or locales is merely coincidence.

Published by Raven Happy Hour LLC
Oxford, MS USA
Raven Happy Hour LLC and all affiliate sites and projects are © Copyrighted 2004-2016

Mandy M. Roth, Online

Mandy loves hearing from readers and can
be found interacting on social media.
(copy & paste links into your browser window)

Website: http://www.MandyRoth.com

Blog: http://www.MandyRoth.com/blog

Facebook: http://www.facebook.com/
AuthorMandyRoth

Twitter: @MandyMRoth

Book Release Newsletter: mandyroth.com/
newsletter.htm

Midnight Echoes: Part of the Immortal Ops Series World (Crimson Ops)

He's a bad-boy vampire feared the world over...

She's off limits...

Vampire and Crimson Operative Bhaltair hasn't always played for the side of good. He's walked a fine line throughout his immortally long life and has very few regrets. He's always had everything he's ever wanted—that is until Meena. As a human descendant to the master vampire he serves, Meena isn't on the menu. That is until he learns he's in danger of losing her to another supernatural male.

Suggested Reading Order of Books Released to Date in the Immortal Ops Series World

This list is NOT up to date. Please check MandyRoth.com for the most current release list.

Immortal Ops
Critical Intelligence
Radar Deception
Strategic Vulnerability
Tactical Magik
Act of Mercy
Administrative Control
Act of Surrender
Broken Communication
Separation Zone
Act of Submission
Damage Report
Act of Command
Wolf's Surrender
The Dragon Shifter's Duty
Midnight Echoes
And more (see Mandy's website & sign up for her newsletter for notification of releases)

Books in each series within the Immortal Ops World.

This list is NOT up to date. To see an updated list of the books within each series under the umbrella of the Immortal Ops World please visit MandyRoth.com. Mandy is always releasing new books within the series world. Sign up for her newsletter at MandyRoth.com to never miss a new release.

You can read each individual series within the world, in whatever order you want...

PSI-Ops
Act of Mercy
Act of Surrender
Act of Submission
Act of Command
Act of Command
And more (see Mandy's website & sign up for her newsletter for notification of releases)

Immortal Ops
Immortal Ops
Critical Intelligence
Radar Deception
Strategic Vulnerability
Tactical Magik
Administrative Control
Separation Zone
And more (see Mandy's website & sign up for her newsletter for notification of releases)

Immortal Outcasts

Broken Communication
Damage Report
And more (see Mandy's website & sign up for her
newsletter for notification of releases)

Shadow Agents
Wolf's Surrender
The Dragon Shifter's Duty
And more (see Mandy's website & sign up for her
newsletter for notification of releases)

Crimson Ops Series

Midnight Echoes
And more (see Mandy's website & sign up for her
newsletter for notification of releases)

**Paranormal Regulators Series and Clear Sight
Division Operatives (Part of the Immortal Ops
World) Coming Soon!**

Praise for Mandy M. Roth's Immortal Ops World

Silver Star Award—*I feel Immortal Ops deserves a Silver Star Award as this book was so flawlessly written with elements of intrigue, suspense and some scorching hot scenes*—Aggie Tsirikas—Just Erotic Romance Reviews

5 Stars—*Immortal Ops is a fascinating short story. The characters just seem to jump out at you. Ms. Roth wrote the main and secondary characters with such depth of emotions and heartfelt compassion I found myself really caring for them*—Susan Holly—Just Erotic Romance Reviews

Immortal Ops packs the action of a Hollywood thriller with the smoldering heat that readers can expect from Ms. Roth. Put it on your hot list…and keep it there! —The Road to Romance

5 Stars—*Her characters are so realistic, I find myself wondering about the fine line between fact and fiction…This was one captivating tale that I did not want to end. Just the right touch of humor*

endeared these characters to me even more—
eCataRomance Reviews

5 Steamy Cups of Coffee—*Combining the world of secret government operations with mythical creatures as if they were an everyday thing, she (Ms. Roth) then has the audacity to make you actually believe it and wonder if there could be some truth to it. I know I did. Nora Roberts once told me that there are some people who are good writers and some who are good storytellers, but the best is a combination of both and I believe Ms. Roth is just that. Mandy Roth never fails to surpass herself*—
coffeetimeromance

Mandy Roth kicks ass in this story—
inthelibraryreview

Chapter One

Meena Emathia sat in the oversized gymnasium that had been built onto her grandparents' home. It was a training facility. To her understanding, it had originally been used solely by her grandfather—a master vampire once feared the world over—and his men. She had a very hard time seeing her grandfather, Labrainn, as a killing machine or a man who struck fear into the hearts of other supernaturals. As far as she knew, he'd given up his wicked ways when he'd mated with her grandmother, a real-life fairy.

And since Meena's birth, even more had changed. Her grandfather had partnered with two organizations, Paranormal Security and Intelligence (PSI) and the Paranormal Regulators. Meena still wasn't clear on the distinction between the two, but she'd been told that PSI was much like the human version of the CIA, and the Regulators were more like a version of the police—but she wasn't totally sure she that was right. She'd once made the mistake of asking for clarification and was still confused as to what went where and with who. Either way, her grandfather and his men all fought for the good guys now.

Her father, Stamatis, was a Paranormal Regulator and had been for centuries. He also worked on and off with PSI directly under their Crimson Sentinel Ops Division (Crimson-Ops), or Fang Gang, as she'd heard his best friend, Whitney—a wolf shifter—joke more than once. Her grandfather's right-hand man, Bhaltair, was also a member of the Fang Gang now, though no one joked with him about the name.

Everyone was smarter than that.

Vampires, werewolves and faerie were commonplace in her world, though she often felt like an outsider looking in. Where most humans had no idea supernaturals existed, and great pains were taken to keep them ignorant of such, Meena had been privy to them since birth. She wasn't like them though.

Not even close.

She glanced around the training room. It was extremely large but relatively empty, as was often the case when her sister Rose was training. Rose had been born with many vampire traits and gifts, but without a demon or the need for blood. This made her special. All the perks with none of the negatives.

Meena wasn't so lucky. Despite both of their parents being supernaturals, Meena had been born human.

A pang of jealousy reared its ugly head, and she was quick to push it down. She didn't like being petty. She was healthy and loved by people who would never grow old and who would more than likely live hundreds of years more than her. They would go on long after she was gone, and that brought her joy. She'd seen a number of her human friends lose loved ones, and the effects on them had been devastating.

She didn't even want to think on it more. Glancing around the training room, Meena watched as Rose flipped, sparring with Bhaltair. At six-two, and second-in-command to her grandfather, Bhaltair was imposing. There didn't seem to be an ounce of him that wasn't muscle. He somehow managed to avoid looking too muscular, but only just barely. He moved with an impressive gracefulness, reminding her more of a dancer than the legendary, feared vampire she'd heard mention of him being more than once. She knew he was holding back.

"Come on, Walt," yelled Rose, annoyance coating her every word. "You're going easy on me. I thought you special operatives were tougher than this."

Meena cringed at the sound of her sister using the English version of Bhaltair's name. It did not suit the man in the least. That didn't stop Rose from calling him Walt or Walter as much as possible. Probably to get a rise out of him.

He didn't take the bait. He did, however, twist and use his fighting staff to sweep Rose's legs out from under her, depositing her on her backside. Meena couldn't help but laugh softly at the look of indignation on her sister's face. The girls often argued, as sisters often did, but in the end they loved each other greatly.

"Jerk move," said Rose, pushing to her feet.

Bhaltair licked his lips, his gaze moving to

Meena for the briefest of moments.

She tensed, her heart rate increasing and her palms beginning to sweat. That response had been happening more and more around him of late. She wasn't sure why, but his very glance could suddenly send her body into overdrive. She wanted to touch him — something she rarely did.

"Have you had enough?" he asked, a Scottish brogue evident. There were times it was quite thick and other times it was barely noticeable.

Rose grunted and went at him again. He deflected her attack with no real effort. That only served to piss Rose off more. Her sister, in addition to possessing the gifts of a supernatural, also had a heck of a temper.

It was important to their parents that the girls be trained and be able to protect themselves should the need arise. Rose had come out of the womb headstrong and ready to kick butt. Meena hadn't, leaving her feeling like a colossal letdown to her parents and the supernatural community in general. She didn't have super strength or excessive speed. She was clumsy at best, and where Rose could take a hit and keep on going, Meena tended to end up battered, bruised or with broken limbs.

When she'd come out the other side of a training session with two broken bones from one well-placed hit by Bhaltair, he'd refused to train her again. She strongly suspected he'd been avoiding her since then as well. The few times he'd allowed himself to be in the same room with her, he'd treated her as if she were a delicate porcelain doll who might break if looked at too long or hard.

For a while, she'd refused to allow it to bother her. She'd stayed busy and done her best to be scarce whenever Rose was training. But lately, Meena was drawn to the training sessions.

More specifically, drawn to Bhaltair. The urge to touch him ate at her, nearly forcing her from her seated position.

She closed the book she'd been reading and watched as Rose swung high at Bhaltair's head with her fighting staff. Meena's breath caught and she waited, fearing he would be hurt. He merely leaned back, the staff gliding past his head as if it had never been a threat at all.

He glanced in her direction and winked.

She was surprised. He wasn't known for winking at her.

Or at all that she knew.

While he was nowhere near as set in the old ways as her grandfather, he was certainly a man out of his time. As an immortal vampire, he'd been alive centuries, and at times, it was glaringly obvious. Not that he looked old or worn, just that his mannerisms and often his lack of pop culture knowledge or modern slang made it painfully clear he was older than he appeared.

Rose lowered her fighting staff and put her hand up. "I've got to go. Hot date tonight."

Bhaltair snorted. "Yer twenty. Too young to date."

Rose undid the tie holding her long, flaming-red hair back. "Dad says the same thing. He wishes I was more like Meena. You know, a bookworm who never gets in to any trouble. Otherwise known as boring."

Meena pursed her lips and pretended the

dig wasn't hurtful. Rose had a long history of speaking before thinking. Meena knew her sister would apologize later, once she'd thought more on what she'd said.

She smoothed her skirt down and avoided looking up for a moment, fearful the moisture pooling in her eyes would be seen. No one liked being called boring. She certainly didn't relish the label cast upon her at an early age. In comparison to Rose, Meena *was* downright boring.

Rose shook her head, raking her gaze over Meena slowly and then wrinkling her nose as if smelling something bad. "Big sister, we have got to get you to wear some sexier clothes. You look like you're ready to attend a funeral at any moment."

Meena surveyed her apparel. It wasn't that bad, was it? The skirt she wore was dark brown, vintage lace with long flowing layers of material beneath it. She had on a matching cami with a black long-sleeved shirt tied loosely over it. The shirt matched her knee-high leather boots.

"Embrace jeans and tight shirts, Meena.

You're always in dresses, and not even sexy, slinky ones. *Boring.*"

Meena pushed her long, unruly dark brown hair behind her ears. Streaks of red danced through it. She envied her sister for having the same color hair as their mother and grandfather. Meena was more of a mix of her mother and father, rather than taking after only one.

Rose approached and tossed her towel at Meena. "Whatcha reading? Poetry again?"

"I don't read poetry...much." She was reading a wonderful book written long ago. When she'd come across it in the archives, she'd had to read it. She couldn't stop herself.

"You live your life in books. College is such a waste of our time. We're on break and you're still studying. I don't get it. Why?"

"You wouldn't understand," Meena said, standing and clutching her book to her chest. Her sister didn't care about learning or soaking up knowledge. Rose only cared about how hard she could hit something. A trait Meena did not share.

"Try me," Rose returned.

Shrugging, Meena made a move to step down from the bleachers but tripped and nearly bit it face first. Bhaltair was suddenly there, catching her, steadying her. Heat flared throughout her body, and she pulled back from him. "Th-thanks."

Rose burst into laughter. "Mom and Dad should have named you Two Left Feet. You are clumsy, hon."

Meena stifled a laugh as well. Rose was correct. She was clumsy.

"Rose, you promised your grandmother you'd visit with her before leaving tonight," Bhaltair said, something off in his voice. He kept Meena close.

That was different and odd, but Meena made no move to pull away.

"Sure thing, Walt," Rose replied as she headed for the doors.

Meena righted herself, her attention on Bhaltair. "How do you not strangle her?"

"I have amazing self-control," he said, making her laugh. He tipped his head, his shoulder-length raven hair falling into his strikingly handsome face. His dark gaze always looked as if he were hiding some big secret, one she wished he'd let her in on. Mostly, she just had to fight to keep from trying to touch the guy, he was *that* alluring. "You were quiet tonight. Is the book yer reading good?"

"Oh, it's really good. It's about the Scottish rebellion in the late 1700s." She stopped, realizing he most likely didn't care.

He lifted a brow. "*Really?* Those were interesting times, to say the least, lass."

"I forget that you lived it." She snorted. His brogue was there, but not as thick as her grandfather's. Bhaltair had been alive during the very time she was reading about. He didn't need her recounting it all.

He'd been there.

"You don't have to pretend to be interested. I'm boring. You can say it. Rose tells me all the time. I think she's a redheaded version of our dad. You know, a total hellion."

Bhaltair chuckled. "Aye, I would agree. She looks much like yer mother but acts most like yer father."

"I'm starting to think I was adopted," she

said, only partially kidding.

He eyed her over. "Yer a green-eyed beauty who is able to take a man's breath with simply a look."

She blushed and lowered her gaze momentarily. "Thank you."

Meena wasn't sure what brought on his statement. Bhaltair wasn't normally known for being overly nice or for handing out compliments. That being said, he must have felt bad for her and maybe even a little bad about ignoring her for so long. Because any man who looked like him and had been alive for centuries certainly wouldn't find her attractive.

Chapter Two

Looking toward the windows, Meena couldn't help but notice how many stars were out. It hit her many times in her life that her father, grandfather, and Bhaltair were never allowed to enjoy the sun. Stars were all they knew now. While she loved the night and had always preferred it to the day, the thought saddened her. "Bhaltair, do you ever wish you were different?"

"How so?"

She shrugged, growing quiet. He eased his hand into hers, standing next to her, and the action felt normal even though they didn't make a habit of holding hands. In fact, she didn't recall a time prior to that night when they'd ever done so.

She didn't care what had brought it on. She just didn't want it to end.

"Are you asking if I miss the sun?" he questioned.

"I'm *sure* you miss it," she said, easing closer to him, her other hand touching his upper arm. She was left leaning against him, holding his hand and touching him, her head resting on his shoulder as they both faced the windows. She stared longingly out at the dark sky, enjoying the closeness to Bhaltair. "I love the night. Stars are so beautiful. So is the moon. It takes my breath away every time I see it full in the night sky. But I can't imagine never seeing the sunrise again. That has to be hard."

Bhaltair stayed silent, but he didn't move away. He remained perfectly still.

Meena caressed his upper arm absentmindedly as she continued to stare out at the night. "It's stunning."

"Aye, *you* are," he said softly.

Sure she'd heard him wrong, Meena glanced up at his profile, her gut tightening at the sight of him there. Everything about the man seemed to ooze power and sex appeal, yet he was always so reserved, so guarded. She lived for the rare moments when she caught a glimpse of him smiling. They were few and far between.

"Tell me your thoughts, Meena," he said, still facing the windows. "I have never been able to read you."

She knew as much, though she wasn't sure why. None of the vampires she knew could read her thoughts. It was the only thing that set her apart from humans. In every other way, she was the same. "I wish I was different. I wish I was more like all of you."

He said nothing as she found herself tearing up. She didn't want to appear pathetic in front of him, but she couldn't seem to stop her emotions as they continued to build.

"I wish I didn't break so easily," she whispered, the words something she'd never spoken out loud before.

"Aye." He tugged her gently until she was standing directly in front of him, still facing forward. He wrapped his arms around her waist, easing against her, his front pressed to her back. "As do I."

She flinched and tried to pull out of his hold. He didn't let go. He held her there gently yet firmly. He was so powerful without even trying that she wouldn't be moving until he permitted it. "Bhaltair, I see the way you all worry about me. I know Grandpa and Dad want to wrap me in a protective bubble. If I could change what I am, I would. I'd be like you. I'd be strong and fearless."

He simply held her, and strangely, it was exactly what she needed. She didn't care what had brought it all on, or why he was doing it. She didn't want it to end. She put her hands over his and rested her head back on his chest.

When he spoke, his deep voice seemed to reverberate through his powerful chest, right into her. "You asked if I wished I were different. I dinnae use to wish for such a thing. I enjoyed being as I am—more than a man. As of late, I often find myself wishing I were more human and less supernatural."

She gasped and twisted in his arms to be able to see his face. "Why? You're perfect as you are."

"You see me as *perfect*?" he asked, his dark brown gaze lingering on her as he eased his hold, allowing her to step out of his grasp. She didn't go far.

She couldn't hide her partial laugh. Was he serious? He was about as perfect as guys came. "Uh, yeah. Do you have a fault? If so, I've never noticed." She held up her hand, ticking off his qualities on her fingers. "You're incredibly loyal and very tender-hearted, even though I think you try to hide that from most people."

He raised a brow quizzically.

"You can pretty much beat up anything that looks at you funny. You know how to deal with both Grandpa and my dad. You're patient. I mean, just the other day Striker was here, but you kept your temper in check, and didn't try to kill him. Even when Grandpa and my dad both went at him. And you've got this nice mix of sophisticated yet funny and free."

Striker, a PSI operative with a thick Scottish accent, and a sense of humor that got him into trouble often, had come by to drop off paperwork for her grandfather. He'd ended up goading her father and her grandfather to the point the two vampires both took swings at the shifter male.

Bhaltair grunted. "I've no patience for Striker. I simply dinnae wish to have to clean his blood from the floors. Should he make another pass at you, I will end him."

Meena smiled up at him, thinking back to

the pickup lines Striker had attempted on her before trying the very same lines on Rose. "Bhal, he's a little too cocky for my liking."

Something she couldn't read passed over his face. "Many women find him verra pleasing to the eye."

Striker was extremely good looking, no question there, but he was no Bhaltair. She loved Bhaltair's darker features and his quiet reserve. She loved how he was sexy without coming off as too sure of himself, and she had always been a sucker for his dark, smoldering gaze. "He's not too shabby, but...well, he's no you."

"No me?" he pressed.

Pink stained her cheeks. She couldn't believe how bold she was being. "I think you're way sexier."

He appeared amused, and she instantly backed away, feeling childlike.

"Forget I said anything. I'll go. I shouldn't be here anyways. It's not like these training sessions are for me."

She tried to go, but he caught her arm lightly. He caressed her flesh with his thumb.

The very feel of his hand on her arm made her breath catch. She closed her eyes faintly, nearly leaning into the feel of him once more. Something about the proximity made her want to submit to him—to surrender fully.

Snap out of it, she thought, but it did little to change her situation. If anything, she pressed against him more. It wasn't as if they did it often—or ever before tonight—but she wanted to be held again by him. She'd always wanted him to touch her in such a way, but she'd never come right out and asked him to. And she never thought he really would.

"Meena, look at me."

The very idea of making eye contact after she'd confessed to thinking he was sexy nearly sent her scrambling from the training facility. She may be human, but she was betting her embarrassment could give her speed that rivaled any vampire's. And if he kept making skin-to-skin contact with her, there was a better-than-average chance she'd show what his touch was doing to her.

"Ask me how it is I see you," he said, still making contact with her.

She paused, the moment's joy fading fast. "I already know. I heard you arguing with Grandma about me once. She was trying to convince you to work with me on self-defense, and you told her I was *too human* for you to bother with."

He stiffened. "You misunderstood my meaning."

"Hard to misunderstand that, don't you think?" The sting of the words still haunted her. She wanted to be like her family. She wanted to be like Bhaltair. Special. Different. Not too human to bother with.

He exhaled slowly. "Meena."

Moisture coated her eyes as she stared up at him. "I need to be on my way. The campus librarian is holding a book for me that I requested, and I promised to pick it up by nine. Night, Bhaltair."

She was also possibly meeting a man there that she didn't want Bhaltair to know about. He wouldn't understand and he'd tell her grandfather and father. And then they'd forbid her from seeing the man anymore. No one really thought much of her visiting the campus library. She did it often enough. It was well known how much she loved it because it was far more than just a regular library. It was magnificent.

The campus library was really a front for one of the many PSI archival departments spread out all over the world. Meena had spent a great deal of time visiting different ones when she was a child and had come to love and appreciate the abundance of history they housed. So many events cataloged. So many artifacts tucked away, kept safely stored under the noses of humans. She loved history, both human and supernatural.

"Meena."

She looked away, unwilling to make eye contact with Bhaltair as a lone tear eased down her cheek. He didn't need to see the effect he had on her. It was bad enough she'd allowed herself to be upset once more with his words of her humanity, spoken months ago. She didn't need to expose herself emotionally to him any more.

A wave of silence swelled steadily between them. Seconds ticked by, each feeling much longer than they were. Still, no one uttered a single word, nor did they pull away from one another. Just when Meena was about to break and fill the deafening silence with idle chatter, Rose burst into the training room.

Her sister was there, standing in the doorway, chomping gum, picking her fingernails, and looking annoyed. "Meena, can you give me a lift to the house? I need to shower and get changed for my date."

"Sure," she said, pulling away from Bhaltair, wiping her cheek as she did. Rose wouldn't understand the tears or why they'd come about. She couldn't relate. She wasn't "too human". "I'm heading past the house as it is."

"Awesome. You're the best, sis."

"Actually," Bhaltair said, his voice slicing through the room. "I was going to ask Meena to remain behind this evening."

Rose perked. "Going to try to teach her to defend herself again, Walter? That didn't end so well the last time."

Meena groaned. "Please stop calling him that."

"Why? It's his name in English," she said.

"But does he really strike you as a Walter?" Meena asked, knowing her sister was just being difficult for the sake of it. "Really?"

Rose grinned. "You're adorable. You defend him all the time." She looked at Bhaltair. "Just yesterday Dad was trying to convince Mom that the world would be better off if you were living in Scotland again instead of ten minutes from us. Meena went nuts. You should have seen it. She told Dad she'd move too if he talked Grandpa into relocating you."

Bhaltair appeared surprised. "Truly?"

"You ready?" Meena asked her sister, wanting away from Bhaltair's questioning gaze. It was no secret that her father and Bhaltair rarely, if ever, saw eye to eye. It was also evident to Rose that Meena had a soft spot for Bhaltair.

Rose's grin widened. She was up to no good. "Sure, but don't you want to know why Walter wants you to hang out here?"

She glanced at Bhaltair. "Maybe later."

"Or, he could come with us. I mean, you never have plans, right? Bet Old Walter there would like to get out."

Meena swallowed hard. While Bhaltair was numerically old, he didn't look a day over thirty. And he never would look any older than that. "Actually, I need to pick up a book at the library and then stop past Carol's."

Rose's face scrunched. "Is Carol making another dress for you? Don't you have enough?"

Meena grinned, but it was forced. She had special plans coming up with a man who she liked, but he wasn't Bhaltair. "This one is for a date."

"Would this date happen to be with the tall, hunky, dark-haired guy I spotted you with a few days back?" her sister inquired.

"Do you skulk in bushes?" Meena asked, only partially joking.

"When I can." Rose smirked. "Tell, tell. Is it the same guy I saw you having coffee with the other evening?"

Blushing, Meena nodded. "Yes."

"And isn't he the same guy I see in the science wing at the university all the time? He a teacher's assistant or something?"

Meena bit her lower lip, sensing Bhaltair staring intensely at her. "Yes, he's in the science wing a lot. He's not a teacher's assistant."

Rose whistled. "Holy crap, Batman, you're dating a professor. Meena, I've never been prouder. He's hot. *Way* hot. Tell me he's dynamite in the sack."

Meena's gaze whipped to Bhaltair. This wasn't a topic she wanted discussed at all, let alone in front of him. She sucked in a deep breath, her cheeks close to the color of her sister's hair. She had to force herself to look away and back to her sister. "Are you ready to go or not?"

Rose pointed, her eyes the size of half-dollars. "Oh, Meena! He is, isn't he? He looks like he would be. I mean, hot with a toned, tight body. He's as big as Bhaltair. Didn't know humans came built that hot."

Meena tensed at the suggestion her date was human.

Her sister caught the movement. "Meena, he is human, right? Dad gave you the giant 'no boys' lecture years ago and then he added the bit that he *might* be willing to permit you to date a human guy since you're so…well, human."

Fighting the urge to tear up once more, Meena stood proud. "It doesn't matter. I'm an adult, and what I do with my spare time is my concern and my concern alone. And I'd appreciate you stopping with the digs about me. I'm painfully aware of what I am and what I'm not. And if I happen to find someone who makes me happy and who doesn't care about my limitations, that is my business. Period."

Rose's jaw dropped. "He's a supernatural?"

Meena grunted but managed a slight nod.

"Sis, he could hurt you." Rose lowered her voice like it would keep the vampire near them from hearing. "Meena, during sex he could accidentally kill you. It's not safe for you to be with a supernatural male. He could rip you to shreds without meaning to."

"Everything comes down to sex with you, doesn't it?"

Rose merely stared at her.

With a shake of her head, Meena attempted to walk away. Rose rushed toward her and touched her. "Dammit, Meena, this is serious. I don't want you hurt. I love you. And Dad would lose his mind if he found out you're seeing a supernatural. Let's be honest, Walter here doesn't look too hip to the idea either."

Bhaltair actually looked like he wanted to snap something in two. Meena hoped it wasn't her. He said nothing as he turned his back to her. For some strange reason, she felt as if she'd betrayed him.

That was absurd. They weren't a couple. Still, seeing Bhaltair's back to her and the way his shoulders were squared left something inside Meena demanding she go to him. That she ease his pain.

She glanced briefly at her sister. "Rose, take my keys and go wait in my car. *Please*."

Her sister didn't protest. She did as asked for once.

Meena touched Bhaltair's back. "Are you going to tell my father?"

"I should." He didn't face her.

"I know, but I'm asking if you're going to?"

"You may nae like Rose's words, but they're true," Bhaltair said. "A supernatural male could hurt you without meaning to. He could kill you when all he wanted to do was love you, lass."

"I don't believe that. If he loves me, he'll find a way to keep from hurting me."

He looked over his shoulder partially. "*I* hurt you, Meena. I broke your bones when I was trying to train you. Do you think I meant to do that?"

She pressed herself against his back and slid her arms around his waist. Without thought, she kissed his back, not once, but twice, before putting her forehead to it. She squeezed him gently and closed her eyes. The action felt totally natural, even though she'd never done anything of the sort with him before. She just had to touch him, to calm him. To keep him from slipping into an angry state. Though she wasn't sure why. "I've never thought you hurt me on purpose."

He stiffened.

She put her cheek to his back, taking full advantage of whatever was happening between them. It felt right. "Bhal, since then, since you figured out I wasn't as sturdy as a supernatural, you haven't harmed me again."

He snorted, his large hands moving over her small ones. "Then see me instead of another supernatural male."

Shocked, she almost believed what he was saying before realizing he was probably trying to ease the tension. She chuckled and kissed his back again. "Thanks for making me laugh. I was worried you'd throw a fit and summon my dad or grandfather."

"The idea of seeing me as more than a friend is humorous?" he asked.

She giggled at the idea that he was being serious. "As if *you'd* ever see *me* as anything more than your best friend's human granddaughter. Let's be honest here. I know how you see me—as too human to bother with. I need to go. Are we all right?"

He cupped her hands gently, squeezing them lightly. "Stay."

"Bhal, I have a book to grab, and then I need to see if my dress fits."

He caressed her hand and her breath

caught.

"Let me take you," he said. "We can spend the night together, running yer errands."

Meena had to struggle to keep from jumping up and down with excitement at the idea he really wanted to spend time with her.

"Doesn't seem very fun for you," she replied, enjoying being pressed against him more than she should. She also grew painfully aware of their size difference. He was massive. She wasn't.

"Let Rose take yer car," he said, sliding one hand up her arm in a way that left a shiver of excitement rushing through her. "We'll take mine."

She found it impossible to deny him or let go of him. "Yes."

He patted her hands. "Guid."

She squeezed before finally finding the resolve to release him. When he turned to face her, she couldn't look away from him. The man was beautiful in the manliest of ways. His lips twitched, and he gave her a partial smile.

Meena couldn't seem to stop herself from reaching up and touching the edges of his mouth. "I love it when you smile."

His smile widened. "While you tell Rose, I'll shower and change," he said, taking a few steps and then stopping, his gaze heated and on her. "Then you can tell me more of this man yer seeing. I wish to meet him."

"Bhal?" she asked, her entire body heating from his smoldering gaze. She shook her head, coming to her senses. "What? No. Why?"

He lifted a brow. "Either allow me to meet him, or I will have no choice but to tell yer father about him. After all, I want you safe. As does he."

Her emotions deflated. "I see."

"Meena."

She averted her gaze. "I'm not feeling so well. I think I'll just skip the errands and head back to my dorm for the night."

He was suddenly before her, his body nearly bumping hers. "Meena, no. Do nae pull away from me."

Confused, she met his stare. "I'm just going to go to my dorm and call it a night."

"No," he said, his hand finding her cheek. "Yer angry with me so you wish distance between us. Yer hurt I'd threaten to tell yer father of the other."

She nodded, blinking back tears.

"Then allow me to meet him so that I do nae worry about you," he said, sliding his arms around her, wrapping her in a large hug. "Set my mind at ease, lass. Please."

She put her palm to his chest and closed her eyes, letting him hold her. "Yes."

"And you will permit me to take you for yer errands on this night?" he asked, one of his hands moving to her hair.

"Yes."

Chapter Three

Bhaltair had to fight with every fiber of his being to keep from lifting Meena in his arms and ravishing her. He had wrestled with the urge to claim her from the moment of her eighteenth birthday, nearly four years prior. Each moment he was permitted close to her was another he suffered in silence, knowing he could not have her. She was not a supernatural. She was not up for grabs, and there was no way he'd earned enough good will with the Powers That Be to have her as his mate. If anything, he'd spent so much of his life playing for the wrong side in the fight between good and evil that he'd probably never be blessed with a mate—a destined love.

There was still the slimmest of hopes that Meena, like her mother, would have latent gifts. Gifts that would show once she was sexually active—as had happened with her mother—but Bhaltair couldn't be the man to test the theory. As much as he wanted to be the one who sank into her tight body and found release in her silken depths, he couldn't. It would be all too easy as a supernatural male to lose control and harm her without meaning to. To break her when all he wanted to do was love her.

He was at war with himself over the matter. He knew he couldn't touch her in such a way, but the idea of permitting another to touch her, sample her, know the pleasures of her body, was too much for him. But if a human male didn't, then Bhaltair would never know if Meena was supernatural as well.

Still, his body ached for her touch, for her closeness. He hated knowing she'd found someone else. That she was now dating. Even the word was horrible. Dating? It sounded so pedestrian. Meena was not a woman one simply dated. She was a woman one wooed. A woman one spent endless hours crafting the perfect poem about, but that would still fail to capture the essence of her beauty. A woman a man would never tire of. She was a gift. And Bhaltair wanted to rip apart the man who dared to think that gift belonged to him. Adding in that the man was supernatural, of all things, infuriated Bhaltair even more.

He had to push his inner demon down as it tried to poke through. It didn't like hearing that she was seeing another man either. Bhaltair was to be feared, for sure, but the demon he carried was far worse. Should Bhaltair permit it freedom and allow it to do as it wished, there was a high likelihood the male Meena was dating would be found dead, missing skin and vital body parts.

Calm yerself, he thought, willing it so.

It took a great deal of effort, but he managed to gain some semblance of control.

When he'd awoken from his daily slumber, Meena had been the first thing he'd thought about. That wasn't rare. What was different was the overwhelming feeling that she was in danger. He'd never felt such a thing before in regards to her and hadn't been able to shake the sensation. He'd been pleased to see her arrive with her sister for Rose's training session. Meena had made herself scarce of late. He knew part of that was his fault—that he'd kept her at arm's length because of how much he'd always wanted her, but he should have realized she was putting distance between them because she had a new man in her life.

A supernatural.

Do nae go into that dark place once more.

Bhaltair kept his wits about him, though he was still unable to let go of the feeling Meena was in danger. The fear had been what had prompted him to ask her to remain behind, to let Rose go on ahead. He had hoped that would ease his unfounded fears. It didn't.

Yer being ridiculous. She is fine. Yer just jealous and overprotective.

He inhaled her sweet scent, cradling her body to his, wanting to hold her this way for all eternity. She had not permitted him this many liberties before, nor had he tried to take them.

"What is taking so long?" The door to the gym opened and Rose appeared, looking annoyed, as usual. She paused, her expression changing somewhat at the sight of them.

When Bhaltair noticed Rose's gaze narrowing, he got the distinct impression she was jealous.

She does nae like sharing my attention, he thought, refusing to release Meena. Rose had always been spoiled. While he was sure Rose had no interest in him sexually, she did want to be the center of attention.

"You fall and skin a knee again, sis?" asked Rose snidely. "That why Walt is holding you and you look like you've been crying? Again."

"Rose," he said in a warning fashion, the overwhelming feeling that Meena was in grave danger returning tenfold. He couldn't permit her to leave. "Take Meena's vehicle and go. I will see to it she gets home."

Rose dropped her bag on the floor. "If she can't drive, I'll drive her home. Thanks."

Meena began to pull away, but he held her in place, planted against him. The look he shot Rose stopped the young woman in her tracks. "You've a date, do you nae? Hurry along."

She squared her shoulders. "I do. Sis, you okay?"

Meena laughed softly. "I'm good."

"Want to tell me what is going on?" asked Rose. "Is everything okay?"

Meena pressed slightly on him. "Everything is great. Really."

"Okay," said Rose as she left the building.

Bhaltair eased his hold on Meena. "I should shower."

"I think you smell perfect," she said.

He nearly laughed, thankful she obviously had something of a pull to him as well. He'd feared it was one-sided. He didn't want to leave her side, but demanding she accompany him to the shower rooms was not an answer. He bent and placed a kiss upon her forehead. "Wait here."

She grabbed his hand. "Bhaltair?"

"Yes."

"This is different tonight, right?" she asked, looking down at their joined hands. "We keep touching a lot."

He nodded. It *was* different for them, but it was how he'd always wished it had been between them. He'd always fought the urge to touch her. "It is different."

"Is it wrong?"

His breath caught. As a loyal subject to her grandfather his response should have been that it *was* wrong—that wasn't what came out of his mouth. "No, Meena. It's exactly as it should be."

She gifted him a smile.
"Wait right here while I shower."
She nodded.

Chapter Four

"Tell me of this man yer seeing," said Bhaltair as he shifted gears in one of the many the expensive sports cars he owned.

Meena pursed her lips and debated how much information he could handle at the moment. From the tense way he was holding himself and driving, she wasn't sure he could handle much in the way of the truth. "He's a professor at the university."

"One of *yer* professors?" he asked, glancing at her briefly.

She shook her head. "No."

"Then how did the two of you meet?" he asked.

She laughed softly, remembering her first encounter with Rudy. "My lab partner needed to drop a paper off to him. She's in his class. Not me. We went past his office and once we stepped in and I saw him, I don't know, it just clicked."

"What clicked?" asked Bhaltair.

"That he wasn't human," she said honestly. "I even blurted out the word 'wolf'."

Bhaltair slammed on the brakes and she went forward, her seat belt holding her in place. He stared straight ahead at the darkened, empty road. "Yer seeing a shifter?"

"Sort of," she murmured. "At first we just spent a lot of time together. He's got an interesting experiment going on at the university. Some privately funded thing for the government. He showed me the labs once, and when we were there, he just sort of kissed me. That was when I realized we'd become something more than friends."

"Are you sleeping with him?" asked Bhaltair, his voice hard.

"No. We're not having relations like that."

"Yet?" questioned Bhaltair, as if sensing she'd left that part off.

She thought briefly about lying but knew better. He'd sense it. "Yet."

"You want to be with him?" he asked, the car not moving still.

"Why are you pushing me so much on this?"

He turned his head to face her, his expression unreadable. "Do you know how most wolf shifters like to have sex? They like to take the person from behind, mount them, drive into them until they are spent, and sometimes they will pin the person to the bed with one hand, pushing on the back of the person's neck. They are known to break beds. They are known to break bones of their *own* kind when having sex. What do you think will become of you, Meena?"

She glanced away.

"Do you think he with forgo his nature for you? Do you think he will resist the urge to mount and pin you? To fuck you until his body is spent? Until yers is broken beyond repair?"

She jerked in her seat, unable to believe he'd said the word fuck to her. She didn't respond.

"Have you nothing to say?" he demanded, making her jolt once more from the power in his voice.

For the first time, she was afraid of him. She faced him slowly, worried what she'd find. "Bhal, are you going to lose it?"

His dark gaze yielded quickly, and he gasped. "Och. No!"

She nodded. "Okay, if you say so."

"Meena," he said, his hand moving to her thigh. "Look at me."

She did.

"I am sorry if I scared you, lass," he said softly. "I've no wish to see you harmed. That is all."

She swallowed hard and decided to tell him everything. "He wants me to chain him."

Bhaltair tightened his grip on her leg slightly. "Come again?"

She found her inner courage and spoke. "He wants me to chain him for our first time together. He wants to be pinned down, shackled really, so that I can do what I want to him, but he can't to me. He thinks it will keep me from being hurt."

Bhaltair opened his hand and flexed his fingers above her leg in the slowest of motions. "This is *his* plan?"

She nodded. "He seems to think if we do that the first time, we wouldn't have to do it again the next time. I guess he thinks he'll somehow get more control."

"Or he believes *you* will gain something

from the encounter," said Bhaltair.

She glanced at him. "Like what?"

He took a deep breath in, and she thought he'd shut down on her. She knew there were things he didn't tell her because he'd been ordered not to. Things her parents and grandparents wanted kept from her. Bhaltair was loyal to a fault.

"Never mind," she said. "I'm guessing this is one of those things you can't tell me because of who you are to my grandfather."

"Aye," he said softly. "It is something I'm forbidden from speaking with you about."

"Why am I not surprised?" As much as she wanted to be angry with him, she knew the rules. She understood vampire politics, and even if Bhaltair was strong enough to overcome the mystical binding that happened when a master vampire gave one of his subordinates a command, he would never break his vow. He had that much honor and respect.

"Meena," he said, his hand coming to her cheek lightly. "I will tell you despite my orders."

She gasped. That was huge. Super huge. All kinds of rules would be broken. The vampire world didn't have shades of gray. It was very black and white. Going against a master vampire could result in death. "No. Bhal, don't get in trouble for me."

"Lass, I'd do anything for you?" He ran a finger over her lip, silencing her with ease. His dark gaze seemed to see right through her. "You may not be as human as you believe."

While the words were clear and she heard them, she couldn't wrap her mind around them.

Of course she was human. What else would she be? The only special power she had was being immune to vampires reading her thoughts. Beyond that, she was as human as they came.

"Meena, because of the Fae in you and the particular line of vampire you come from, you may have hidden gifts that are special to your line of vampire, but not to all," he said, leaning in, his face close to hers. "Gifts that, should you have them, will only manifest after you have been sexually active. We do nae know for sure, but we believe this is because of the type of Fae yer grandmother is and, as I said, the line of vampires you hail from. Am I right to assume yer a virgin still?"

She nodded slightly, not entirely at ease with the topic of the conversation. Most women her age had been sexually active. Meena had never had much interest in the opposite sex, or sex at all for that matter. At least, not until she'd turned eighteen. From that point on, her sexual appetite had emerged and focused primarily on Bhaltair. She'd been doing her best to direct it at someone else, but still, in the end, it was Bhaltair she thought about in that way.

"That is why I believe your friend wishes to be chained for yer first encounter, but thinks future ones will nae require such steps," he said, his words clipped, his shoulders back. "What I wish to discern is how he knows you may have latent gifts when you, yerself, have no idea."

Meena was still stuck on the part about possibly not being human. "Hold on. You're saying if I have sex, I may be more like Rose and Mom? Less like me? Less *too* human?"

"There is no way to know," he said.

She stared at him blankly. "Uh, yeah, there is. I could have sex."

His expression hardened. "You want yer wolf that bad?"

"What?" she asked in disbelief.

"You want to fuck the wolf?" he demanded.

Puzzled, she stared at him. "Bhaltair?"

His nostrils flared, and his eyes pooled with liquid darkness, a sign he was no longer the one in charge. His demon now was.

She'd heard all the stories of just how bad his demon was in its heyday. She wasn't naïve enough to think it had totally changed its ways. If it was pushing up and taking charge so quickly, that meant Bhaltair, the man she cared for and trusted, wasn't pulling his own strings.

A demon was.

Gasping, Meena thrust herself against the car door, fear beating at her from the inside out. While she'd grown up with vampires all around her, and was even the product of more than one, she knew enough to realize they could be deadly. She'd never seen Bhaltair's demon rise. He'd kept that side of himself from her.

Seeing his face begin to contort, his eyes become black abysses, shook her to her very core. She tried to steady her breathing, having been told again and again by Bhaltair himself when he used to train her, that supernaturals got excited when they caught the scent of human fear. All the training and all the preparations in the world meant nothing when she found herself face-to-face with the one man she wanted more than any other, all while his demon took the proverbial wheel.

"You want him," he said, a flash of fang showing.

She froze. What was he talking about? Who did she want?

As he reached for her, she jerked, her pulse racing, her fear growing. His fingernails lengthened and nearly connected with her. A second before he would have made contact, he blinked and his face returned to normal instantly. The black in his eyes receded. He lifted his hands, holding them to both sides of himself, his nails returning to normal. "Meena."

She remained perfectly still, unsure what had set him off or if it would happen once more. "Bhal?"

He cleared his throat and turned to face forward in his seat. He put the car in gear, pulled back onto the road and drove without speaking or even blinking. The rest of the ride to the university went by without him uttering a sound. When he pulled to a stop in a parking lot that was as close to the campus library as he was going to be able to get, Meena touched the door handle, her stomach in a knotted mess, her nerves on edge.

Bhaltair made a move to reach for her and then stopped mid-motion, worry filling his eyes. "Can I touch you?"

"Y-yes," she answered, her voice betraying her.

He put his hand on her leg gently. "Meena, lass."

She glanced at him unhurriedly, worried about making any sudden movements that might set him off once more.

"I'm so verra sorry I lost control in front of you like that," he said, caressing her thigh affectionately. "I dinnae mean to scare you."

"But you did scare me," she returned, her gaze going to his hand on her leg. "I've never seen you like that before."

"I know."

She refused to look at him. "I asked Dad to show me his vampire side once, but he wouldn't. Grandma made Grandpa show me his. He wasn't happy to do it, but he did."

"Aye, I remember," said Bhaltair. "You were only eight at the time and insisted on seeing what all the fuss was about. Though, you dinnae seem frightened of Labrainn's vampire side at all then, lass."

"I wasn't," she replied, exhaling softly. "Because I knew he wouldn't hurt me."

"But you were nae sure if I would," he grunted.

She met his gaze. "You got really mad, really fast. I shouldn't have confided in you. I'm sorry. I thought...I thought we were friends."

"Lass," he said, lifting his hand and going for her cheek. "I never wanted you to see that side of me. If I could take it back, I would. I wish that you could see me as just a man. Not a monster."

Meena gasped and twisted in her seat. She made a move to hug him, but her seat belt locked her in place. She struggled and managed to undo it. She touched Bhaltair's face. "You're not a monster."

"I'm nae a man," he said evenly.

"But you acted like a jealous one," she said without thought. As the words sat between them, filling the space, she gasped. She'd just blatantly accused him of having feelings for her. "I didn't mean that. I'm sorry."

"Och, lass. Do nae apologize, especially when yer right," he countered, his hand going over hers. "I was jealous of you and yer lover."

"Bhal, Rudy is not my lover."

His lip curled. "His name is Rudy? That is a horrible name."

She laughed mellifluously, still touching his face. "Bhaltair isn't exactly commonplace."

"Guid point."

She smiled. "Are we okay? You and me?"

"Aye."

"I'm going to grab my book. Try not to turn all vampire-y while I'm gone. Okay?"

Bhaltair glanced past her into the darkness, in the direction of a dimly lit streetlamp. He cupped her hand, pulling it from his face. "Meena, do you trust me?"

"Yes."

"If I were to tell you that my gut says to let the book be on this night, to just allow me to take you home, would you?" he asked, apprehension evident.

She couldn't recall a time she'd seen him this way. He looked stripped bare before her, his emotions there for her to witness. "Bhal?"

"Would you trust me, lass?" he questioned, a note of desperation clinging in the air between them.

"What's wrong?"

"I do nae know. But my gut, my demon, and my heart says to nae let you out of my sight tonight."

His heart?

"Thank you for worrying about me," she

said, using her free hand to touch his muscular chest. Even through his dress shirt she could feel the hardness of his body, and it excited her. "I'm safe. I come here all the time at night. The librarian is a record keeper for PSI. Really nice woman. I promise I'll be fine, and you're right here. If I have a problem, I can call you from my cell phone. It would take you two seconds to do your vampire thing and get to me."

"My vampire thing?"

She grinned. "The speed and leaping tall buildings gig."

He snorted. "Ah. I see. No."

"No? What do you mean no? You don't leap-tall-buildings? I've seen you guys fly before. It's really cool. Not cape-and-tights cool, but cool all the same."

He cocked his head to the side, appearing somewhat lost in the conversation. She wasn't surprised. Slang often got lost on him. "No. I do nae like the idea of letting you go in there alone. I'll go as well."

Her breath hitched at the idea of dragging Bhaltair into the library with her. Rudy had promised to meet her there, and the last person she wanted Bhaltair around was Rudy. She didn't need Bhaltair flipping out and going into full vamp mode again. "I'm good. Never mind. I don't need the book."

His gaze narrowed, suspicion showing in his expression. "Meena, why are you suddenly so compliant?"

"No reason," she said a bit too fast to sound believable. "We should go."

His jaw set. "Because yer worried yer lover will be there too. You do nae want me around him."

She cringed. "He's not my lover. But yes, Rudy knew I needed to stop there tonight. He mentioned he'd try to meet me. I'm early so he might not be there yet, but still. Considering how *great* you took the idea of me being with him, it might be best you avoid going in too."

Bhaltair was out of the car in the blink of an eye.

Meena raced after him as he headed directly for the path to the library. She caught his arm. "What are you doing?"

"Getting a book," he said sternly. "I know how much they mean to you. I'd nae want you missing out on any."

She tugged on him to no avail. "Bhaltair, stop."

He did, but he didn't look pleased.

"Go back and sit in the car."

"No."

Her jaw dropped. "Wow. Jerk."

His eyes widened. "Meena?"

She sighed. "Fine, but if you start a fight, I will never forgive you."

His jaw set and his shoulders squared, but he nodded all the same. "Aye. I'll behave."

Chapter Five

Bhaltair glared around the massive building, looking for any signs of the man Meena was dating. He found none. Aside from a short, plump woman with a head of white hair and glasses thicker than soda bottles, he and Meena were the only ones in the place. Her would-be-lover was a no-show and dammit to hell if she didn't look pleased by the notion. All he wanted to do was get the man alone long enough to stress he was never to even look upon Meena again, let alone think to bed her.

Och, you want to pluck out his eyes and then skin him alive. There would be no talking. Only killing.

He grinned at the thought.

Soon, he was so swept up in the fantasy of torturing a man he'd never met, that he didn't notice the new scents rushing in around him. It wasn't until his demon reared up, demanding he take heed, that he paid attention.

Shifters.

Not just shifters.

Something else too.

Vampires?

The scents made no sense to him. They were convoluted and mixed with something else.

Death.

Had he not just read over reports that Striker, a fellow PSI operative, had dropped off regarding an emergence of a new enemy, he'd have never put together what the smell was. It was the scent of rotting flesh, vampire and shifter all in one. The report had labeled them bastard hybrid genetic manipulation attempts —experiments gone horribly wrong. They apparently had a limited shelf life, the trials and tests causing them to die a slow death, but not before they were used to their fullest potential. The report also made note of just how powerful they were. And they were here now closing in on someone.

His heart raced as he realized who that someone was.

Meena.

They were moving in on her location as she browsed a section of books about history, the book she'd come for already in hand, but she had decided she wanted more. As much as he'd wanted to keep her from the facility because of his gut feeling, he found it impossible to deny her the very thing she loved so much — books.

Bhaltair's gaze whipped to the older woman at the counter as the smells intensified all around him. She looked up from her desk, lowered her glasses, met his gaze, and nodded.

"Do what you must," she said. "I've tripped the alarm. Help will be here soon."

He didn't hesitate. He drew upon his vampire speed and was with Meena in an instant. She gasped and dropped the book she'd been holding.

"Bhal," she said, shaking her head. "You really need to make more noise when you move. You scared me."

The second she bent to retrieve the book, the shelf exploded in front of her, a clawed hand thrusting through from the other side.

Bhaltair deflected the hand, knocking wide the assailant's attempt to strike Meena. He shoved her to the side with his foot as gently as he could, but he accidently made her tumble over. Meena collided with the wall and his gut clenched. He ripped the would-be attacker through the shelf, causing more books to fall all around him.

The thing he dragged through to him didn't look like anything he'd ever seen before. It smelled heavily of death, had the eyes of a vampire, but the jaws of a shifter as it snapped at him. Its skin was a pale grayish blue with large bruises all over it and several puss-filled sores.

He punched the hybrid so hard that he splintered its nose into its brain. Hopefully, sending bone fragments through its brain wasn't something a hybrid could heal. But to be safe, he broke the hybrid's neck as well. He wouldn't risk Meena.

He allowed the hybrid's limp body to fall to the floor. A split second later, another hybrid came bounding over a shelf at the end of the row. The hybrid did a cross between a run and a gallop at him, foaming at the mouth. Its sights were set on Meena.

Bhaltair's demon roared up, in perfect

understanding with the man.

Anything that attempted to harm his woman would die.

Chapter Six

Meena tried to make sense of what was happening. One second she'd been happily browsing through books in the secret PSI section of the library, and the next the shelf had seemed to come alive. Now everything on her hurt.

She rubbed the back of her head and pushed up and off the floor. Her gaze whipped to the blur of forms before her. It took her vision a moment to adjust, and she realized she must have taken a knock to the head. When she was finally able to see straight, the first thing she saw was Bhaltair slamming his fist into the face of some sort of creature. It dropped away quickly and then lay there motionless.

She was almost to her feet when she caught sight of another creature leaping down the aisle at them.

In the past, she'd spent endless hours pouring through PSI archives. They kept records of all kinds of supernaturals. She'd never seen anything like what was attacking them. And she'd seen some sketches of some pretty hideous-looking demons.

Bhaltair didn't seem fazed. He crouched and then slammed his body into the creature, lifting it up and off the ground. The force of the collision shook the area. Meena glanced to the side just in time to see what remained of the massive bookshelf coming at her.

Lifting her arms, she tried to deflect the giant shelf, but it didn't work. The shelf hit her arm and she felt the bone snap like a twig before the entire weight of the unit was on her, thrusting her back against the very wall she'd only just managed to get up from. Thankfully, the wall caught the shelf, and kept it from crushing her, though everything on her hurt as if an anvil had dropped on her.

She clutched her arm to her chest. She crawled as best she could in the direction of Bhaltair and the creature he was fighting. She knew enough about Bhaltair to know he'd win the fight, and she also knew she didn't want to be far from him.

Something snatched hold of her ankle, ripping her backward, out from under the collapsed shelf and away from Bhaltair.

Away from safety.

A scream tore free from her as she was flipped over by another monster. This one somehow managed to be uglier than the other two. It stared down at her from eyes that reminded her of Bhaltair's when his vampire had taken over his actions. Was the thing part vampire?

It leaned in, inhaling deeply before licking her temple. She froze in terror and horror as its hot breath peppered over her face. Spittle from it dripped down her cheek, and she fought the urge to retch. It brought a clawed hand to her other cheek and she lay there, helplessly trapped beneath it, her broken arm wedged between her and the monster.

"M-Meena," it said in a voice that was barely understandable.

The thing knew her name?

She shrieked and tried to no avail to push it from her. Pain shot through her arm, and she cried out again. "Get off me!"

It didn't budge. It did, however, begin to grind against her in a sexual manner, and she dug deep for a resolve that shocked even her.

With mustered courage, Meena slammed her head into the creature's.

It hurt beyond words and she nearly blacked out from the pain, but it was enough to momentarily stun the thing on her. She used the distraction and rammed her knee upward, hitting its groin.

It rolled to the side, and she scrambled out from under his hold, her broken arm still pressed tightly to her as she tried once more to crawl under the downed shelf, in the direction she last knew Bhaltair to be.

The creature growled and then grabbed her by the leg, its claws sinking into the flesh of her thigh. She didn't need to look at her leg to know it had caused a massive amount of damage. She cried out again and glanced up as the sounds of scratching metal filled the area.

The collapsed shelving unit was propelled in the other direction and Bhaltair was suddenly there, his face contorted into that of his vampire side, his eyes pooling with black and his attention on her. She held no fear of him. In that moment, his demon was more than welcome. It meant he was pissed and alive.

Bhaltair hissed and leaped up and over her. She couldn't see where he landed, nor could she follow his speed with her naked eye. The weight of the creature was ripped free from her, and she turned as best she could, everything on her screaming in agony.

"She is *mine*!" yelled Bhaltair, his voice significantly deeper than normal. He lifted the creature that had said her name high in the air by its throat. Bhaltair tipped his head, the action looking very preternatural. He twisted and slammed the creature into the wall, pummeling his hand through the monster's face.

Bhaltair's shoulders heaved as his gaze snapped to her, his eyes still black. She knew she probably should be afraid of his vampire side—it was a trained killer and was technically a demon—but she didn't fear him. He focused on her leg. She looked down as well and for a minute it felt as if all around her slowed. Time seemed to pause as she stared at the mangled mess that had once been her leg—

the massive amount of blood spurting from her thigh soaking the library floor.

I'm in shock.

Bhaltair reached for her but was ripped back by another of the creatures. Meena tried to focus on what was happening, but she couldn't keep her eyes open. She'd never been so tired in all her life. The pain ebbed away, and she closed her eyes, knowing deep down that Bhaltair would do what needed to be done.

He'd protect her.

Suddenly, something brushed over the side of her face and she tensed, scared to look and see what that something might be. Already she'd seen creatures that would haunt her nightmares. She wasn't sure she could take much more.

"Lass, 'tis me," said Bhaltair, his voice never sounding so sweet.

Meena reached for him, and he caught hold of her and held her close. She broke down, sobbing hysterically as she clung to him.

"They are no more, Meena." He looked down at her leg and then surprised her by biting his wrist. He met her gaze. "Do you understand what I must do?"

She did. Her father had tried to heal a cut she'd gotten the same way when she was younger. His blood should have healed her instantly, but it hadn't. It hadn't done anything. "It won't work."

He held his wrist over the open wounds of her leg and allowed his blood to drip into them freely. "Lass, you've lost too much blood. Without me trying, I do nae know that you will survive me seeking medical attention for you. And I cannae lose you."

Meena closed her eyes a second, feeling faint, knowing she was losing far too much blood. She opened her eyes just in time to find Bhaltair's lips near hers. Surprised, she gasped and he captured her mouth with his.

The kiss was somehow exactly what she required in that moment. She needed her mind on anything but the shock and horror that had happened. On anything other than the pain and what she was sure would be death with all the blood she was losing.

As his tongue eased around hers, her body

warmed. It was Meena who increased the heat level of the kiss, devouring his mouth. She nicked her tongue on one of his fangs. There was a flash of pain and then the strangest of feelings started deep in her gut. It felt as if someone was there, pulling elastic bands back and forth between them, hooking her to Bhaltair, and he to her.

Bhaltair showed her who was in charge of the kiss, and it wasn't her by any means. She gave in to him as he orchestrated the event. The pull between them forced her to ease closer to him, not that she needed encouragement.

"Mine," he said, breaking the kiss only for a second before going at her mouth once more.

Mine, she thought, the word dancing around her head, her body humming with building energy. She'd all but forgotten about the attack. About everything that had happened. It wasn't until she leaned back and her hand slid through a puddle of congealing blood that it all hit her.

Gasping, she broke the kiss, her eyes wide. "Bhaltair?"

He lifted her off the floor and held her close. The look on his face was one she couldn't read. The way he held her let her know she was now safe. That no one would harm her.

There was a swooshing noise followed quickly by a booming male voice. One she knew well. "What the fuck happened? Meena? Baby girl?"

"Daddy?" she asked, surprised he was there.

"I summoned him," said Bhaltair, making no move to set her down or hand her over to her father.

Meena stayed pressed against Bhaltair but glanced over at her father, Stamatis. His eyes were wide as he stared at the carnage around them. The section of the library they stood in was like the aftermath of a war zone. The more she soaked it all in, the harder she cried.

Her father snapped out of his stupor and reached for her. "Meena!"

She whimpered but shoved herself tightly against Bhaltair, unwilling to leave the safety and comfort he provided.

Her father, looking more like a badass biker than a secret operative, stepped closer. Worry etched his face as he came just shy of touching her broken arm.

"Sweetie, this is broken and you're bleeding," he said, his voice deepening as he spoke. "What happened?"

She continued to cry too hard to answer him, but as she glanced down at her injured leg, she realized that while it was still bleeding, it was doing so slowly, and from a wound that looked small compared to what it had been when it first happened, only moments ago. Had Bhaltair's blood helped to heal her to some degree?

Bhaltair cleared his throat. "She was attacked by a group of hybrids."

"While you were with her?" her father demanded, narrowing his gaze. He rivaled Bhaltair in size and strength. If the two went to blows, they'd both end up harmed. "How the hell could you let her be hurt?"

"Daddy, no," she managed. "This isn't his fault. He asked me to trust his gut feeling and not come in here tonight. I thought he was being silly and overprotective. I should have listened to him. Now look at all the books that are destroyed because of me."

Her father looked puzzled. "Meena, you're crying over books?"

She nodded and cried harder.

Bhaltair kissed her temple, the action drawing the attention of her father at once. Bhaltair didn't seem to care. "Lass, I'm sure most can be repaired."

She perked. "Really?"

Tossing his hands in the air, her father grumbled and then bent, examining the closest of the creature's bodies. His face was ashen as he met Bhaltair's gaze. "These things came after my daughter?"

"Aye, Stamatis, I do nae think it was a random attack."

Her father, known more for being a cocky smartass than a man who shared his emotions, looked visibly shaken by the ordeal. "Bhaltair, thank you for protecting her. I'll get her to Aine."

There was a commotion at the other end of the room and the librarian appeared, holding a rather medieval-looking weapon in one hand as she pointed at Whitney—her father's best friend and fellow Paranormal Regulator—with her other hand. Whitney, a wolf shifter who stood well over six foot, and while sinewy, still managed to be packed full of muscle, looked scared of the tiny woman.

The librarian jabbed him with the weapon. "You'll be bringing that overdue book back, bucko."

"Yes, ma'am," Whitney replied, hurrying in their direction.

The librarian cleared her throat, his gaze narrowing in on Bhaltair. "Vampire, I just got off the line with PSI. No alarm alert came through on their end. Someone disabled the system. The techs are working on it. And one of the two security men is dead. Found his body when I went to check the alarm system. The other is missing."

Meena gasped. The library didn't have everyday, run-of-the-mill security. They trained operatives. She twisted and stared down from Bhaltair's arms at the creature near her father's feet. These things had killed a PSI operative? The reality that they could have killed Bhaltair hit her hard.

She reached for his chest—realizing a beat later, at the almost complete absence of pain, that it was with her broken arm. In fact, it was feeling better and better by the minute. "Are you hurt?"

Her father grunted. "He's fine. Stop mollycoddling him. And you," he said to Bhaltair, "hand me my daughter."

Whitney came to a stop near her father. Their features were vastly different. Where Meena's father had jet-black hair and a goatee, Whitney had long sandy-blond hair with streaks of platinum through it. He had a five o'clock shadow, which was more facial hair than she was used to seeing on him. His blue eyes widened as he sniffed the air. "I smell wolf shifter in this mix, but it's tainted. Wrong."

"Aye," Bhaltair replied. "I believe two hybrids are a wolf and vampire mix. They reek of death and decay, so it's hard to tell."

Whitney tipped his head to Stamatis. "Anyone want to tell me why that dickhead is holding Meena and why you're letting him?"

Her father groaned. "Because my baby girl is refusing to let me take her."

Bhaltair snarled, glaring at Whitney. "Make any attempt to remove her from me, *wolf*, and I will kill you. She is *mine*."

Meena jerked as her father and Whitney gasped. Whitney grabbed for her father, ripping him back as he started to charge at Bhaltair. "Whoa, no. Calm down there, big guy. No killing the dickhead just because he laid verbal claim to your baby."

Meena tensed. "I'm not his baby. Rose is. I'm a grown woman. And…wait. What? Verbal claim?" She wanted to say more but the dull throb that had been in her head increased tenfold. She clutched her stomach. "I'm going to be sick."

"So am I," snapped her father. "You are not his mate, Meena! No."

"What?" she asked, her stomach cramping more.

"Stamatis, this is nae the time nor place to argue. Meena requires medical attention," said Bhaltair.

Whitney whistled low. "I did not see that claim coming. Nope."

Chapter Seven

Meena sat on the exam table in a clinic that catered to supernaturals, with her father near her, pacing endlessly. Whitney was matching him step for step, more than likely tired of playing referee between her father and Bhaltair.

It had been an ordeal to simply agree on transportation to the facility. Her father had wanted her to ride with him. Bhaltair had refused to put her down, and Meena had been thankful for that. It was Whitney who'd finally pointed out that they were wasting time with petty arguments that could be better spent getting her medical attention.

Bhaltair was close, his hand near hers on the table. She inched her fingers over his and kept her head bent. Making contact with him felt right, and she needed to feel normal—to feel safe. She'd wanted to ask him about the verbal claiming Whitney had mentioned, but she couldn't seem to find the right words. The car ride over had been silent, his mood foul after arguing with her father.

Dr. Sambora, a supernatural himself, reentered the room. He had her chart in his hands. He was handsome and smart, though often he lacked a lot in the way of a sense of humor.

She sighed. "Can I go now? I'm fine."

And she was. Her leg was now healed over fully. Her arm was still sore, and Dr. Sambora had claimed the films showed it wasn't broken, despite her knowing deep down that it had been at the library.

"Meena, did one of them bite you?" Dr. Sambora asked.

Her father was in front of her in an instant, his eyes wide. "Meena?"

Whitney had to drag him backward. "Dude, relax, and let the doctor do his thing."

Bhaltair took her hand entirely in his, seemingly unconcerned if he set her father off again. "I shared my blood with her, if that is what yer getting at?"

Meena tilted her head, holding Bhaltair's hand tighter. "I shared mine with him too. When he kissed me, I think I cut my tongue on his fangs."

"You kissed her and exchanged blood with her?" Her father went nuts. It took Whitney *and* the doctor to get him backed against the wall. He pointed at Bhaltair. "I will kill you."

"Daddy," she said, jerking upright. "Enough. Bhaltair saved my life, and if you're going to keep acting like a child every time anything is brought up, then you are going to have to leave the room until Mom gets here. You're ancient. I expected better of you."

He blinked and lifted a brow.

Whitney failed to hide his laugh.

Dr. Sambora faced her and released her father. "If I can continue. Meena, there are anomalies in your blood work that weren't there at your last checkup a year ago. PSI's labs are sending me the results of the tests they're doing on the hybrids that attacked you."

Her father stepped away from the wall. "What kind of anomalies? Is she infected with whatever it was that turned them into what they are?"

"No," the doctor said. "Well, I don't think so."

It was Bhaltair who leaped up and began

to yell. "You do nae *think* so? What the hell kind of response is that? I will nae lose my woman to whatever those were. Fix her now." He yanked Dr. Sambora up until his feet cleared the ground, and it wasn't as if Sambora was a weak or frail man.

Meena gasped, and her father grabbed Bhaltair, pulling him free of the doctor. "Calm down."

Whitney caught Meena's gaze and grinned wide. "Bet you never thought you'd see the day your father was the voice of reason, huh?"

She knew Whitney was trying to lighten the mood, and she appreciated it. She glanced down at her leg. "The minute Bhaltair shared his blood with me, my leg started to heal. That didn't happen when Dad did it long ago. The wound didn't heal instantly like Bhaltair's or Dad's would if they were injured, but it healed fast enough to watch it happen. And by the time I got here, it was just a scratch. Now it's smooth skin. Why did it work with Bhaltair, but not my own father?"

Dr. Sambora took a step back and glanced at the ceiling. A sure sign he knew the answer, but didn't want to say.

Whitney twisted and motioned to Bhaltair. "Holy shit, you really *are* her mate!"

Her father put his head in his hands. "This is not happening."

Meena stared at Bhaltair, waiting for him to say something. He merely glanced away. She flexed her arm, the very one that had been broken at the library. It was nearly healed as well. "Why do you keep calling me your woman? And why do you keep saying I'm yours? You've said the word *mine* more than once tonight. And why is Whitney saying we're mates? I know what mates are. I grew up around supernaturals all my life. If we were mates, we'd have already figured that out long ago, right?"

He said nothing and refused to look at her.

She tensed.

Whitney hooted. "Hot damn, I think Dickhead did figure it out, at least on some level. How long have you known?"

The muscles in Bhaltair's neck twitched. "We're nae mates. We can't be."

Hearing his rejection stung more than it

should. She wrapped her arms around herself and lowered her head. He didn't want her.

"Meena," her father said tenderly. "I fucking hate him. Say the word and I'll kill him. I can see how upset his words made you."

"What happened here?"

Meena glanced up as her grandmother, a full-blooded Fae, came rushing into the exam room. Thankfully the facility catered to supernaturals, so it had oversized rooms. They'd have never all fit in a normal one. Meena wasn't sure how old Aine really was, all she knew was that her grandmother looked like she was in her twenties and always would. She was also very petite but packed a lot of power in that small frame.

Her long, wild red curls bounced about as she hurried toward Meena, brushing right past Stamatis.

"Oh, sweetheart, I heard whispers from the trees of an attack on someone I love. The minute I put together that it was you, I feared the worst. Nature made it seem as if you were on death's doorstep. You don't look bad. A bit roughed up, but certainly not as if you're dying."

Meena gulped and glanced at Bhaltair, then back at her grandmother. "It was really bad, Grandma. I'm pretty sure I was going to bleed out on the spot. Bhaltair saved me."

A large, rather knowing smile spread over Aine's face. "Did he now?"

Meena knew the woman well. She was up to something. She reached out fast, taking hold of Aine's wrist. "Grandma, no. Don't make a bigger deal of this than it is. Bhaltair only did what he did because he's Grandpa's second-in-command. There isn't anything more there. He's made it very clear that I'm not his special someone, and you already know he sees me as too human to bother with."

Bhaltair grunted. "Meena."

Aine continued to smile in Bhaltair's direction. "Is that so? You don't see her as your special someone? Odd. I could have sworn you saw her as a mate, as nature had intended, but that you were simply too stubborn and bullheaded to realize as much. And each time you did begin to suspect, you talked yourself out of it because of your loyalty to my husband. So, really, I always just thought you were an idiot when it came to my granddaughter and something of a coward in regards to your feelings for her, but what do I know?"

Meena jerked. "Grandma?"

Aine focused on her. "You've been through a lot on this night. And I can sense your hurt and pain with Bhaltair. What happened?"

Meena didn't respond. She didn't have to.

"Dickhead just stated very publically that she isn't his mate. So while she got a verbal claim in one breath from him, he rejected that claim in another," stated Whitney, his normal lighthearted approach to things missing from his words. "Stamatis isn't going to have to kill the dickhead. I'm going to do it for him. If you're lucky enough to find your mate after being alive for centuries, you don't fucking reject her. You don't push her away for anything."

"Oh, sweet wolf," said Aine, compassion in her voice. "All of you stubborn alpha males think that, right up until you meet your mates. Then the stupid kicks in and look what we're left dealing with. Men. Natural-born morons."

Meena shook her head. "I'm not Bhaltair's anything. And he's not my anything. Can we stop talking about this now? It's weird enough that I kissed him and the whole *mine* thing. Can we just let it go?"

Aine narrowed her gaze. "What whole *mine* thing?"

Meena glanced at the floor, already knowing that while vampires couldn't read her mind, Aine could.

Aine gasped and then clapped. "Oh, Bhaltair, you did it! You exchanged blood with her and laid verbal claim to her during a heightened state of passion? I always wondered if the addition of Stamatis's line of vampire would alter how the girls' claims would work. I see it did. They apparently do not require the full act of sex for a claim to stand. They simply need the blood exchange, the passionate moment, and the verbal claim to all happen together."

Meena tensed. "Grandma, would that explain the elastic bands I felt forming between him and me? Why I felt like I was being connected to him mystically?"

Her father eased closer to her, looking like he was dying to say something. He moved past Aine and drew her into his large, powerful embrace. "Baby girl, I'm so sorry that you were attacked. I'm sorry I wasn't there to protect you. And I'm sorry that asshole of a mate you have is being this way to you. Also, I'm sorry *he's* your mate."

"Pretty sure Labrainn feels the same in regards to you being his daughter's mate," said Whitney from the sidelines. "Megan is his baby girl and there is no way he's happy she got you as a mate. Shocked he isn't here forcing me to hold him back from Dickhead too."

Aine nodded. "But Stamatis is slowly growing on him. I believe my husband is not here now because Bhaltair has blocked the events of tonight from him. They share a deep connection, and I believe Bhaltair, whether aware of it or not, understood my husband's fierce need to protect his granddaughter would have outweighed his common sense. He'd have forced the two of them apart, much like I'm sure you want to do, Stamatis."

Her father hugged her tighter. "I want to gut the prick, but right now I'm only worried about my baby girl."

Meena squeezed him. "Daddy, I'm fine. Bhaltair did what all of you would have wanted him to. He protected me, and he saved my life. Please be nice to him. It's okay that we're not mates. That doesn't make him a bad person. It just means he's not the man for me."

Aine perked. "And who is the man for you? A certain tall good-looking wolf shifter?"

Her father whipped around and pointed at Whitney. "Touch my daughter, and I'll rip your fucking throat out."

Whitney paled. "Hey, I would never dream of it!"

Aine laughed. "Not him. Rudy."

She knew about Rudy?

Meena yelped. "Rudy! He was going to meet me at the library, but he never came. Ohmygod, those things might have attacked him too. We have to go back. We have to look for him."

Bhaltair snarled. "I do nae care if yer wolf was eaten by them. Yer nae going back there and yer nae to see him again. Am I clear?"

"Oh, look, he can speak," added Aine with a wink. "Does someone not like the idea of Meena with another man? Is someone jealous?"

"Grandma, how do you know about Rudy?" asked Meena, easing out of her father's hold and standing. Her clothing was covered in blood and ripped up. She knew she looked a mess, but she didn't care.

Aine flashed a knowing smile. "There isn't much I'm unaware of."

"He might be hurt. Make them go and check. Please."

Her father formed a T with his hands. "Hold up. Her wolf? Rudy? What the fuck is a Rudy? Explain."

Whitney pulled a chair out from near a small desk and straddled it. "This is getting good."

Meena made a move to head to the door, but she wasn't quite as fully recovered as she'd first thought. She fell forward, and her father and Bhaltair lunged for her. Bhaltair beat her father to her, dragging her to his chest and steadying her.

She stared up at him. "You have to help him."

Chapter Eight

Bhaltair found himself holding Meena close, wanting to whisk her far away and bed her. He wanted all the things having her as a mate promised. But they were not to be. She couldn't really be his. Aine was mistaken. It was rare, but it happened. And Meena was only worried about her shifter. Nothing more. "Meena, he wanted to bed you, lass. I'll nae help him. I'll kill him with my bare hands."

Her father roared, "He wanted to what?"

Whitney beamed wider from his seated position. "Seriously, this gets better and better."

Meena pushed out of Bhaltair's hold, hurt flashing in her green eyes. "At least he wanted me."

Bhaltair wanted her more than he'd ever wanted anything. How could she not know as much? "Do you nae think if I could, I'd be the man to take you? To show you endless pleasures? To lose myself in you? To make you mine for all eternity?"

Her mouth fell open, and she stared at him. He was a bit shocked by his words as well, so he couldn't blame her, but they were the truth, and he wouldn't take them back. Grinning slightly, he touched her chin with his index finger and closed her gaping mouth. He ran his finger over her lips. "Lass, you cannae possibly think I do nae share the pull to you? That I do nae want you?"

Her look said that was exactly what she thought.

Foolish woman.

He continued to trace his finger over her mouth. "I serve yer grandfather, and yer father would nae be pleased with me either if I acted on my feelings for you."

"No. I would not," Stamatis said from the side of the room, surprisingly standing on his own, not being held back. "But I'm smart enough to know when it's out of my control, and if Aine is saying what I think she's saying, it's really fucking out of my control."

"Daddy, I'm not his mate. I'm human," protested Meena.

Dr. Sambora cleared his throat. "About that. As I was saying before, Meena, the anomalies in your blood are anything but human. I wouldn't classify you as human any longer."

Aine clapped once more. "Oh goodie! It worked. When Bhaltair claimed you, it triggered your latent gifts."

Bhaltair's gaze whipped to the fairy. "She's pure, untouched by man. She's nae come into her powers."

"Bhaltair, you are stubborn and blind when it comes to my granddaughter. You always have been. And you really don't listen very well. I clearly stated sex wasn't a requirement for everyone." Aine approached, tugged on him, making him bend, and then she kissed his cheek. "I love you and, in time, her father will come to terms with what was decided long ago."

"Do nae speak in riddles, woman. She is nae mine," he said, his anger growing, his demon threatening to come forward. "I love her with all of me, and to tempt me with the possibility of a future with her is beyond cruel."

"You love me?" asked Meena, digging her fingers in to his side.

"Bhaltair, on my honor, she is yours. I've known since Megan was expecting her, but I knew better than to speak the words out loud for fear I would change destiny," replied Aine. "You and Meena have always been mates. She just needed to come of age for you to be able to claim her as your own, and you've done as much now."

"I dinnae bed her," he said, holding his woman in his arms. "I wanted to, Aine, I still do, but I would never disrespect Labrainn so."

"I know. You've said as much. It's easy to see that you're struggling so much with all of this that you're missing so much of what is going on. I stand by my alpha males are morons when they meet their mates statement." Aine smiled. "You're so loyal to my husband that it's clouding your judgment and your thoughts. And I believe that is what has *really* kept you from claiming Meena before now—when she turned eighteen. Your blood exchange, coupled with your verbal claim and the kiss was what the two of you required. You can bed her later. That is a bonus. And my husband has no say in the matter now. The claim is done. I can sense Meena's powers growing as we speak."

Confused, he shook his head. "I was under the impression Meena would only come into her powers if she were to be sexually active. And there was only a slim chance even then that she'd have any latent gifts."

Aine winked. "There is always a workaround, old friend, and you found it."

He stared blankly at Aine, positive the fairy had lost her mind. Aine had sat everyone down when Megan, Meena's mother, had come into her gifts, explaining how that came to be — because Megan wasn't fully Fae, her powers remained latent until she became of age and sexually active. No one ever mentioned workarounds.

Aine laughed, her focus on him. "You look so lost, Bhaltair."

He moved his hands over Meena's arm, searching for signs of injury. There were none. Aine had been correct. Meena was healed, and that meant she was coming in to her powers. "I do nae understand."

"Take her with you. Keep her close. I

suspect many changes are going to be coming at her from all directions. She'd want you to be the one with her. No one else." She faced Stamatis. "Do not fight him on this, or you will lose your daughter forever. She will be forced to choose between her father and her mate. In the end, a father cannot win that choice."

Stamatis moved closer, took a deep breath, and extended his hand to Bhaltair. "I guess this means we're family now. I still think you're an asshole."

"Och, I do nae like you much either." He took Stamatis's hand and shook it.

The two men nodded and then Meena rushed at her father and hugged him. "Daddy, thank you for being nice to him. But between you and me, I think Grandma has gone around the bend. I'm not Bhal's mate. But I do like seeing the two of you get along."

Stamatis kissed the top of her head. "Stay with Bhaltair for now, Meena. Do not return to your dorm, our home or your grandparents'. I'm not going to risk you being attacked again. I've got Regulators on campus now working with PSI to track down leads. We will check on this Rudy guy. Not you. Not Bhaltair. I want him close to you at all times."

Whitney stood and grinned. "You do realize he's going to shag your daughter, right?"

Stamatis twisted and punched his friend in the jaw.

Whitney grinned and rubbed the spot. "Worth it."

Aine groaned and then looked at Dr. Sambora. "You seem quiet."

"Happy to see one of us find their mate," he said, his voice somber. There was a story there for sure. "I'll leave you all to this. I'm going to go run more tests on Meena's blood."

Aine headed to the door. "Bhaltair, take her to your farm. She'll be safe with you there. And stop being so afraid of your demon side around her. It loves her too. Oh, and congratulations on the union. Megan and I will plan a party to celebrate it."

Meena gulped. "She is so weird. Can I shower, and does someone have clothes I can change into?"

Whitney turned and grabbed a set of

surgical scrubs Sambora had brought in earlier. "Here. Doc gave you these. There is a shower at the end of the hall."

"Thank you."

Chapter Nine

Bhaltair drew his car to a stop outside the two-hundred-year-old farmhouse and cut the engine. Meena hadn't stirred on their journey to the safe location. She'd fallen asleep in the car after saying very little to him. He'd listened carefully for sounds of her breathing and heart rate the entire drive. He still wasn't sure what Aine was up to, but his demon trusted her logic.

That should have been enough to send him screaming in the other direction. For centuries after he'd first been turned into a vampire, his control over his demon had come via Labrainn's assistance. Labrainn had been powerful enough to help control Bhaltair's newly sired self.

He doubted highly that Labrainn could control him now. No. Bhaltair could have been a master vampire himself long ago, but he'd stayed by Labrainn's side out of loyalty. The man's do-gooder ways had annoyed Bhaltair at first. And truth be told, Bhaltair had not cared much for Aine in the beginning, believing her to have cast a spell over his master. But he'd eventually learned the truth. The only spell cast was that of love and mates.

Nothing nefarious.

And with one kiss to Labrainn, Aine had managed to reform not only him, but Bhaltair and the other vampires loyal to the man. The big bad vampire and his men ended their wicked ways, pulled out of the view of others, and began living and acting as though they were mere humans. They had lived lives away from any who had known them when they'd ruled by fear for so long that Bhaltair had become used to deceit for the greater good. That was why he'd purchased the farm, set out on the edges of Labrainn's territory. The farm had been barely standing when Bhaltair had driven past it and felt a sense of calling and duty to return it to its once glory days.

And he'd spent over twenty years doing just that. As he thought about when he'd made the offer and bought the farm and all the land on it, he stiffened.

He'd done so when Megan was expecting Meena.

His gaze snapped to Meena. Often when he'd sneak away to work on the farm, he would think of one day residing there with a family of his own. Of what it would be like to see children filling the halls, laughing, playing and filling the home with joy, as a home was meant to be. In recent years, since she'd come of age, Bhaltair would envision Meena there as well, her belly swollen with his child as he chased around their other ones.

He shouldn't have been surprised Aine knew of his farm renovations and that it was now inhabitable. He'd not told anyone that he'd been working on it. She was that powerful. Hell, the bloody woman probably knew of his desires to have Meena live with him and grow large with his babes.

It was a fantasy he clung to, desperate for it to be true, though he'd known it never could be. Yet here she was, with him at the farm, showing signs of being more than human. He didn't dare hope Aine was right—that they were mated now and she was his for eternity. He couldn't. There was no way he'd be able to stand thinking he could live his dreams only to find that not to be the case. It would crush him, and in the end he knew his demon would win the internal struggle, and he didn't want that.

He didn't want to be evil again.

"You want her," he said softly, still gazing upon Meena's beautiful face as she slept in the seat next to him.

He took a deep breath and then exited the vehicle, heading around and getting Meena as well. She never stirred as he carried her sleeping form over the threshold of what he had always viewed as their future home. Though none who knew him would believe it. They saw him as a man with too much money, a mansion, and countless cars and expensive toys. They did not see him as a man who lived on a historic farm, painstakingly returning it to its original state, but with modern amenities.

Something about it had called to him. Much like Meena and the way she had always called to him. Without thought, he lifted her higher in his arms as he headed up the stairs. He kissed her forehead, his body tightening with need for her.

She whimpered and twisted against him.

"Bhal?"

"Sleep, my love," he said, and tensed.

My love?

He nearly missed a step. A small chuckle broke free from him. He would need to be renamed Two Left Feet at the rate he was going around Meena.

As he reached the top of the staircase, he headed for the master bedroom. He'd redone the entire home with UV-protected windows and plantation shutters. In addition, he'd hung thermal curtains to add yet another layer of protection from the sun's harmful rays. He also made sure to keep a fresh stock of blood on hand, for long nights when he worked on the grounds. He'd been restoring one of the three barns on the property over the course of the last few months—stealing away whenever he had free time.

Bhaltair carried Meena to the king-size bed and laid her gently on it. He was about to walk away and leave her to rest while he made her a cup of tea when he noticed her shoes were still on. He removed them slowly, careful to not wake her, still unsure how she'd managed to heal herself by merely having a blood exchange with him.

Was Aine right?

Meena turned, her dark hair fanning out around her on the white pillow. Her ruby-red lips parted slightly, and it took all his control to avoid bending and sampling them. He wanted her more than he'd ever wanted anything in his immortally long life. Hunger for her lanced through him, bringing his demon forward and nearly to the surface.

Staggering away from the edge of the bed, Bhaltair gasped and held up his hands as if to defend himself from what lay within him. "No. I'll nae allow harm to come to her."

He nearly drew upon his vampire speed to run out into the night and put as much distance between himself and Meena as he could, but that wasn't what happened.

His demon didn't want blood.

No.

It wanted sex.

With Meena.

Bhaltair shook his head, desperate to cling to control. He forced himself away from her more and found himself at the doorway to the master bathroom. He hurried into the bathroom and splashed cold water on his face, his hands going to the edges of the sink as he bent his head. He had not struggled with control like this for centuries.

Why now?

Why with Meena?

She is your mate. Aine is right.

With a gasp, he froze. No. He would have known sooner, right? He had heard Labrainn speak of Aine and how he'd known upon first glance that he wanted to make the woman his. Stamatis and Megan had wasted very little time joining after meeting. The few other vampires he knew with mates all claimed their women quickly after crossing paths with them.

A sobering thought came over him. Each of them had met their significant others when the women were already of an age to be claimed. Bhaltair had known Meena since she was but a babe in her mother's womb. Had something inborn kept him from seeing her as a mate while she grew to be an adult woman?

Was that why he'd struggled so with his

desires for her once she'd become of claiming age? Was Aine right?

"No," he said, his voice hoarse. She wasn't his, and to allow such foolish notions to enter his mind, even to merely entertain them, would cause him to unravel. Whatever was happening between them was a fluke. It would sort itself out, so long as he kept himself from doing anything stupid, such as walking into the other room and kissing her, like he wanted desperately to do.

"Bhaltair?" she asked, her voice cutting through his thoughts.

He wasted no time moving quickly to the side of the bed. She looked up at him with wide eyes. "Where are we?"

"Yer safe. I've nae heard anything of yer would-be-lover. I can go and check in. I know you wish to be with him and nae here with me."

She moved with a speed that stunned him. Speed she should not have as she launched herself off the bed and at him.

He caught her around the waist. She wrapped her arms around him and held him, shaking in his arms.

He was powerless to do anything other than return her embrace. "I'm so verra sorry, lass. I should have never allowed harm to befall you, and I should have gone in search of yer Rudy the moment you requested it of me. Once we know the threat to you is no more, I'll take my leave of you, and I will be the one to suggest to Labrainn that I be sent to Scotland to oversee affairs there."

She leaned back, and the next he knew, she hauled off and slapped him across the face with enough force to actually make it sting.

He gasped, and she glared at him. "Don't you dare talk about leaving me again. You think my sister is a hellion, you just watch, mister. I'll show you what a woman on a rampage looks like if you dare try to leave me. I will not have my mate on the other side of the world. Understand me?"

Bhaltair heard her words, but the pull of her lips moving was too much for him to resist. In one quick motion, he captured her mouth with his, thrusting his tongue into her mouth, silencing her instantly.

She went limp in his arms, her tongue greeting his in return.

He knew he should release her and put distance between them, but he couldn't. He found himself carrying her toward the wall, ravishing her mouth the entire way. Bhaltair pressed her body against the wall. He ground against her, wanting to be one with her.

She ripped at his shirt, exposing his chest. Bhaltair could barely think, let alone stop himself as he took her wrists, pulling her hands from him, the press of his body keeping hers pinned to the wall.

"Bhal," she whispered, biting at his lower lip.

He shook as he fought for control of his raging need for her. "Meena, lass, I want you, but I do nae want to hurt you."

She writhed against him, tipping her head back, exposing her neck to him. The temptation to sink his fangs into her creamy flesh was so great he wasn't sure how he managed to avoid doing just that.

He was about to release her when white light burst free from her, bathing him and the room.

Instincts nearly had him diving out of the way, fearful the light would be as the sun's rays were to him—deadly. But he couldn't leave her. He held her as she cried out, the light dimming quickly, her gaze filled with confusion.

Inhaling, Bhaltair smelled it then—power. It was raw and thick all around them. It reminded him slightly of Aine's, but it also had trace elements of vampire as well.

Meena struggled against his hold on her wrist. To his shock, she broke free. She grabbed his face, power still riding the air between them.

"Now," she said, something off in her voice. "Take me now."

"M-Meena, no," he returned, desperately wanting to give her what she wanted.

In the blink of an eye, she was standing on her own, thrusting him backward, in the direction of the bed. Bhaltair hit it with such force he was surprised the frame didn't buckle and break.

Meena moved at him with a speed that

rivaled a vampire's. She shook her head, worry crossing her face. He knew then she wasn't in control of what was happening to her, and it scared her as much as the events surprised him. He caught her gently, dragging her down on top of him.

"I've got you, love."

"Bhal," she said against his ear, her nipples hard and easy to feel even through the material of her shirt. "What is happening?"

Every bit of doubt he had on if she was his mate or not, and if he'd claimed her vanished. He knew then Aine's words were true. Meena was his.

"Yer nae human, lass. Yer my mate, my wife, and yer coming into yer full powers. Do nae be scared. I'm right here with you. Just let me love you."

He barrel-rolled with her, putting himself on top. He touched her neck gently and then dipped his head, his mouth finding hers. Their kiss was tender, yet full of need. He broke the kiss long enough to speak. "I'll be gentle with you, Meena. You have my word."

She grabbed for him, kissing him with a

hunger that made him smile against her lips. She wanted him too, and that meant the world to him. He skimmed his hands down her torso and eased them up and under the surgical scrub top she wore, exposing her bare breasts to him. His cock hardened to the point he was sure he would come then and there. Meena writhed under his touch, responding to him with ease.

"Yer mine, lass. All mine."

Chapter Ten

Meena tipped her head to the side as Bhaltair's mouth closed over her nipple. She'd never felt so much pleasure before and thought for sure she'd burst from it. He managed to make her body burn even more when he rolled his tongue around her nipple as he ground his lower region against hers.

"Bhal," she whispered, running her hands through his hair, holding him to her breast. His fangs nicked her nipple, and a flash of pain raced through her, followed quickly by pleasure as Bhaltair began to suck. He increased his movements against her, grinding his clothed erection against her mound, causing liquid to pool at the apex of her thighs.

Meena arched her back, countering his movements, wanting more than he was offering. She wanted all of him, and he was taking far too long to get to the good parts. She whimpered, his name falling from her pursed lips once more.

He eased off her, taking the pleasure as he went. He undressed before her, giving her a show as he undid the buttons of his shirt and slid it off. The man was chiseled perfection, and her mouth watered at the sight of him. When he got to his belt, her eyes widened, and the edges of his lips quirked upward slowly. He knew the effect he was having on her.

She didn't care. She wanted all of him and fast.

Lifting a hand, she reached for him, but he shook his head, easing his pants open, his long, thick cock breaking free and bobbing in the air. He was huge, and she wanted to touch him, taste him, feel him.

Meena attempted to sit up, but he was suddenly over her again, his clothing fully discarded, his naked body against her. He hooked a finger into the top of the scrub bottoms she wore and met her gaze. Flecks of black began to swim through his irises, and she knew he was fighting his vampire side. She didn't care.

"Love me," she said.

"Aye, lass. I intend to." He lowered his head and trailed a line of kisses down to the top of the scrub bottoms. Using his teeth,

Bhaltair tugged her bottoms down her body inch by painfully slow inch until they were off. She thought for sure she'd combust as he kissed her bare inner thighs, shoving them apart, leaving her pussy exposed to him.

Bhaltair growled and dipped his head, burying his face between her legs. Meena nearly came up and off the bed as he swiped his tongue over her clit. She gasped, her legs falling open more. He thrust a finger into her tight, wet channel, and it hurt at first, as he broke through her virgin barrier. She flinched, and Bhaltair increased his licks against her clit, chasing away the pain. Meena wasn't sure how her body managed to adjust to his finger, but it did. Within seconds, he had another finger added to the mix, stretching her more and more.

Glancing down the length of herself, she met his hot, smoldering gaze. She'd never felt so free before, so wanton, and she loved every second of it. She touched the side of his head. "I love you."

He lifted off her pussy, his chin glistening with the proof of just how much she enjoyed his actions. His gaze narrowed as he moved up and over her, clutching his erection with one hand. He lined up with her core and steadied himself with one arm above her. "I love you too, lass."

She ran her hands up his arms and over his back. He stared down at her, passion burning in his dark eyes. His cock nudged at her thigh. She gasped at the feel and the size of it, convinced something so large would never fit into her.

His kisses came faster. She clung to him, opening her legs wider for him to settle between her thighs. He was too much, too big. Meena's first reaction was to push him off, but her legs wrapped around his waist as if they were no longer taking signals from her brain. They wanted all of him. Her hips were next, swiveling under him as he began to inch slowly in and out of her.

Before she knew it, they'd struck a rhythm together, and the pain ebbed away. He plunged into her like a piston, hammering her body to the bed in a most delicious manner. She moaned, pleasure racing through her. He pumped harder, drilling into her, and she clung to him as pleasure built.

"Yes!" she cried as the muscles in her legs began to tighten, and her stomach quickened.

He kissed her, and she felt his fangs increasing in size. Their mouths followed the same erotic dance as their bodies, kissing, loving, exploring. Breaking the kiss, she offered Bhaltair her neck, knowing deep down that the vampire side of him craved the act as much as it did sex. She wanted him happy and fulfilled. Wanted to give her mate what he required.

Bhaltair drew away from her mouth and locked gazes with her. "Do you accept me?"

"Yes," she whispered.

He struck, snake-like, at her neck.

There was no pain. Only pleasure that crashed over her, making her legs quiver. Bhaltair jerked above her, his body going rigid. His head remained down, and she knew he was still biting her neck, drinking from her.

She ran her hands into his hair. "Mine," she whispered. The pleasure reached new levels and she cried out, her body shaking beneath him as she orgasmed. The pleasure surged through her lower regions and she cried out, grabbing a handful of his hair with one hand and raking her nails down his back with the other. Her hips erupted in uncontrollable undulations as her pussy spasmed around his cock. Bhaltair thrust in deep, his fangs still in her neck, as his body tensed. She knew he was coming in her, filling her with his seed.

Meena eased her hold on his hair and kissed his temple as he drew off her neck and licked the area he'd bitten. He stayed rooted deep in her body. "Meena, did I harm you?"

Her eyes widened a second before she found herself laughing. "Ohmygod, if that was your idea of hurting me, do it again."

He offered a bad-boy smile. "With pleasure, my love."

She touched his cheek. "Are you okay with the idea of me being your mate? I know I'm not what you originally wanted."

Bhaltair stayed above her. "Meena, look around at this house. I bought it for you, for us, long ago. And even though the dream of you and me together here seemed like a fantasy that could never happen, I know now I've spent the last twenty plus years preparing for you to be my wife. I'm sorry I was too stubborn to admit that fact."

She lifted the hand she'd raked down his back and noticed blood on her fingers. "Sorry."

He waggled his brows. "Do nae apologize. Blood turns me on even more."

She gulped. "I was kidding about doing it again. I need a few minutes. You're a big guy and it was my first time."

"I love you," he said, kissing her tenderly.

Chapter Eleven

Bhaltair stood behind his wife as she sat in a chair in the living room of the farmhouse. Labrainn and Stamatis stood opposite him, both looking less than pleased to see him touching Meena. Aine, who was between the two vampires, couldn't seem to stop smiling. Megan, who was sitting on the sofa, looked happy as well.

Megan spoke. "How does it feel to be someone's wife?"

Meena took a deep breath, moving her hand over Bhaltair's on her shoulder. "Good. Really good, Mom. Tell me the truth, how many times did Dad threaten to kill my husband?"

Megan snorted. "I lost count around fifty. Your grandfather was worse."

Labrainn huffed. "She's just a babe. Too young to wed."

"Dad, I mated with Stamatis around the same age," said Megan.

Labrainn gave Stamatis a hard stare. "Do nae remind me."

Whitney entered and glanced around. "Nice place. They tell me it's yours."

"Ours," said Bhaltair, rubbing his wife's shoulders tenderly. "What have you learned of the attack on Meena?"

Whitney continued. "It was planned. We tracked the hybrids' trails back to a lab on campus."

Meena gasped. "Rudy's lab?"

Labrainn locked gazes with Bhaltair, and he felt the familiar tug of his master's voice in his mind. *Who is this Rudy?*

A man who thought he could dare touch my woman.

Stamatis stepped forward. "Sweetheart, Rudy was one of the hybrids. Sambora came to the scene and verified the tests PSI was doing. Rudy was one of the hybrids that Bhaltair killed."

Meena looked up at him and he waited, expecting his mate to be angry with him. She sighed. "One of them knew my name. That was him, wasn't it?"

"More than likely, my love."

She stiffened. "I'm so sorry I brought that

into your life."

She was sorry?

Bhaltair moved around, stood before her and bent, taking her hands in his. "Meena, you dinnae bring anything bad into my life."

Whitney cleared his throat. "PSI thinks Rudy was working for some place they call the Corporation. From the sounds of it, the thing is evil to the bone."

Meena closed her eyes and a lone tear fell down her cheek. "I'm so sorry, Bhal. I should have known."

"Lass, do nae weep. I will be forced to seek out a voodoo priestess and raise Rudy from the dead so that I can kill him again."

"I would be glad to help," said Labrainn.

"Me too," added Stamatis.

Aine laughed. "Look. They can all agree on something for once."

"Just wait until Meena tells us she's expecting a baby," added Whitney. "I bet Stamatis and Labrainn agree on trying to kill Bhaltair for touching her."

"Aye," said Labrainn.

Stamatis glared at Bhaltair. "Don't even

think of touching her like that."

"Too late," said Aine in a singsong voice, fluttering past her husband, right at Meena. "I can sense Meena's power all over her, and with it, I sense a child taking hold in her. It would appear the union will be blessed."

Bhaltair barely heard Labrainn and Stamatis as he registered what Aine was saying.

He was to be a father.

He lifted Meena out of the chair, held her to him and kissed her passionately, knowing he'd never let her go again.

THE END

Immortal Ops Series Helper

Immortal Ops (I-Ops) Team Members

Lukian Vlakhusha: Alpha-Dog-One. Team captain, werewolf, King of the Lycans. Book: Immortal Ops (Immortal Ops)

Geoffroi (Roi) Majors: Alpha-Dog-Two. Second-in-command, werewolf, blood-bound brother to Lukian. Book: Critical Intelligence (Immortal Ops)

Doctor Thaddeus Green: Bravo-Dog-One. Scientist, tech guru, werepanther. Book: Radar Deception (Immortal Ops)

Jonathon (Jon) Reynell: Bravo-Dog-Two. Sniper, weretiger. Book: Separation Zone (Immortal Ops)

Wilson Rousseau: Bravo-Dog-Three. Resident smart-ass, wererat. Book: Strategic Vulnerability (Immortal Ops)

Eadan Daly: Alpha-Dog-Three. PSI-Op and handler on loan to the I-Ops to round out the team, Fae. Book: Tactical Magik (Immortal Ops)

Colonel Asher Brooks: Chief of

Operations and point person for the Immortal Ops Team. Book: Administrative Control (Immortal Ops)

Paranormal Security and Intelligence (PSI) Operatives

General Jack C. Newman: Director of Operations for PSI North American Division, werelion. Adoptive father of Missy Carter-Majors.

Duke Marlow: PSI-Operative, werewolf. Book: Act of Mercy (PSI-Ops)

Doctor James (Jimmy) Hagen: PSI-Operative, werewolf. Took a ten-year hiatus from PSI. Book: Act of Surrender (PSI-Ops)

Striker (Dougal) McCracken: PSI-Operative, werewolf.

Miles (Boomer) Walsh: PSI-Operative, werepanther. Book: Act of Submission (PSI-Ops).

Captain Corbin Jones: Operations coordinator and captain for PSI-Ops Team Five, werelion. Book: Act of Command (PSI-Ops)

Malik (Tut) Nasser: PSI-Operative, (PSI-Ops).

Colonel Ulric Lovett: Director of Operations, PSI-London Division.

Dr. Sambora: PSI-Operative, (PSI-Ops).

Immortal Outcasts

Casey Black: I-Ops test subject, werewolf. Book: Broken Communication.

Weston Carol: I-Ops test subject, werebear. Book: Damage Report.

Bane Antonov: I-Ops test subject, weregorilla.

Shadow Agents

Bradley Durant: PSI-Ops: Shadow Agent Division, werewolf. Book: Wolf's Surrender.

Ezra: PSI-Ops: Shadow Agent Division, dragon-shifter.

Caesar: PSI-Ops: Shadow Agent Division, werewolf.

Crimson Ops Division

Bhaltair: Crimson-Ops: Fang Gang, vampire. Book: Midnight Echoes.

Labrainn: Crimson-Ops: Fang Gang, vampire.

Paranormal Regulators

Stamatis Emathia: Paranormal Regulator, vampire.

Whitney: Paranormal Regulator, werewolf.

Miscellaneous

Culann of the Council: Father to Kimberly. Badass Fae.

Pierre Molyneux: Master vampire bent on creating a race of super soldiers. Hides behind being a famous art dealer in order to launder money.

Gisbert Krauss: Mad scientist who wants to create a master race of supernaturals.

Walter Helmuth: Head of Seattle's paranormal underground. In league with

Molyneux and Krauss.

Dr. Lakeland Matthews: Scientist, vital role in the creation of a successful Immortal Ops Team. Father to Peren Matthews.

Dr. Bertrand: Mad scientist with Donavon Dynamics Corporation (The Corporation).

Dear Reader

Did you enjoy this title and want to know more about Mandy M. Roth, her pen names and all the titles she has available for purchase (over 100)?

About Mandy:

New York Times & *USA TODAY* Bestselling Author Mandy M. Roth is a self-proclaimed Goonie, loves 80s music and movies and wishes leg warmers would come back into fashion. She also thinks the movie The Breakfast Club should be mandatory viewing for...okay, everyone. When she's not dancing around her office to the sounds of the 80s or writing books, she can be found designing book covers for New York publishers, small presses, and indie authors.

Learn More:

To learn more about Mandy and her pen names, please visit http://www.mandyroth.com

For latest news about Mandy's newest

releases and sales subscribe to her newsletter
http://www.mandyroth.com/newsletter/
To join Mandy's Facebook Reader Group: The Roth Heads, please visit
https://www.facebook.com/groups/ MandyRothReaders/

Review this title:
Please let others know if you enjoyed this title. Consider leaving an honest review on the vendor site in which you purchased this title. Reviews help to spread the word and boost overall sales. This means more books in the series you love.

Thank you!

Made in the USA
Columbia, SC
27 October 2023

25085228R00083